Teresha Rue-Hughes

Where is Sungi Bear?

Illustrated by Doina Paraschiv

This book belongs to: _____

Published in the United States by Sungi Bear LLC

For further information:
Email: sungibear@gmail.com
Visit us at www.Sungibear.com

The Sungi Bear Collection
Book No. 1
Where is Sungi Bear?
Summary: Sungi Bear is playing his favorite game of hide and seek with his mom and his cat Friskus.

ISBN #9780998848303

Printed in the United States of America

The Sungi Bear Collection

Dedication

*This book is dedicated to my sons Sundiata
"Sungi Bear", Eshawn and Sa'id. You always inspire me.
Thank you. I love you very much.*

Sungi Bear loves bedtime stories. His mom is the best storyteller.
She makes everything so exciting, and this makes
Sungi Bear very happy. Friskus, the cat seems
to enjoy the stories too.

Sungi Bear also loves to play hide and seek.
He could play hide and seek all day long.

One night, when his mom finished reading the bedtime story,
Sungi Bear yelled, "Mommy, you can't find me!"

According to Sungi Bear, this meant it was time to play hide and
seek. Sungi Bear's mom also loves to play hide and seek, but she
always seems to have a hard time finding him.

"Now where did my Sungi Bear go that quickly?"
Sungi Bear's mom asks Friskus. "He was just here!"
The cat is baffled too, so both of them start to look
for Sungi Bear.
"I think the first place we should look is under his bed," says
Sungi Bear's mom, "That's his favorite hiding spot."

Is Sungi Bear hiding under the bed?

Nope! No Sungi Bear there.

"I know how my Sungi Bear likes to pretend his closet is a spaceship that zips him to the moon. What do you say Friskus? Should we look there?" Sungi Bear's mom wonders.
The cat is all for it, so they eagerly walk to the closet.

Is Sungi Bear hiding in the closet?

Nope! Sungi Bear is not in there.

Mama Bear turned around, "You know what, Friskus? Sometimes, when Sungi Bear is tired, he likes to sit in my reading chair. He says it rocks like a sailboat and that helps him go to sleep faster." So they hurry to check the reading chair.

Is Sungi Bear hiding behind the reading chair?

Nope! No Sungi Bear there.

The cat then runs over to Sungi Bear's step stool.
"Aha! You're right, Friskus," mama Bear exclaims. "Sungi Bear likes to
pretend his step stool is Mt. Everest and he is climbing to the top.
Did you know Mt. Everest is the tallest mountain in the world?
I just know for certain that he will be there!"

Is Sungi Bear hiding under the step stool?

Nope! Sungi Bear is not there.

"Hmm..." said Sungi Bear's mom, "Sungi Bear loves to gaze out at the stars at night. One night he spotted the Big Dipper...

Maybe he's hiding behind the curtains."

So she creeps over to the window and gently but swiftly pulls the curtains open.

But there was no Sungi Bear there.

Next, Sungi Bear's mom asks the cat, "Friskus, do you remember how Sungi Bear likes to get into the clothes' hamper and pretend to be laundry, so he can surprise us? I wonder if he's hiding in the clothes' hamper today. What do you think?"

Nope! No Sungi Bear there.
Phew! Someone needs to do the laundry soon.

Next, they look all around the room to see where else Sungi Bear could be hiding. Sungi Bear's mom has an idea: "Hey! What about his toy chest? Sungi Bear loves to play with his big construction trucks and fast race cars."

Is Sungi Bear hiding in the toy chest?

Nope! Sungi Bear is not in there.

"Friskus," asks mama Bear, "Do you think Sungi Bear could be hiding behind his favorite raincoat that is hanging on the coat rack? He does like to wrap it around himself like it's a superhero's cape."

Nope! No Sungi Bear there.

"Well, it was worth a try, right?" sighed mama Bear.

At this point, Sungi Bear gets a bit impatient, lets out a loud giggle and yells, "Mommy, hurry up and find me!"

"Now, I just heard your voice but I still can't seem to find you, Sungi Bear," his mom responds. "Friskus, where do you think he is?" The cat doesn't have a clue.

"Sungi Bear once said he wishes he could shrink and fit inside a backpack," mama Bear thought out loud. "That would be cool, right?" Friskus agreed, so they went to check it out.

Nope! Sungi Bear is not in there.

"Since Sungi Bear is not hiding in the backpack, behind the curtains, or in the clothes' hamper, where else could he be?" Then mama Bear remembers, "He loves to draw fun pictures! He could be hiding behind his drawing board."

Is Sungi Bear behind the drawing board?

Nope! No Sungi Bear there.

Still unable to find Sungi Bear, they then go over
to his alphabet floor mat. "Perhaps Sungi Bear is pretending to be
a mouse and is hiding under the mat," his mom suggests.
This got Friskus excited.
"Relax Friskus! I'm just joking!" exclaims his mom. They peek under
the alphabet mat anyway, just to be sure.

Is Sungi Bear hiding under the alphabet floor mat?

Nope! Sungi Bear is not there.

Finally, after searching everywhere, Sungi Bear's mom cries out, "I know what will make a cool hiding spot! Behind Sungi Bear's dresser!" She rushes over, with Friskus in tow.

Is Sungi Bear hiding behind the dresser?

Nope! No Sungi Bear there.

"Ok Sungi Bear, we have checked everywhere; where can you be?"
his mom asks, smiling. She turns to the cat,
"Help me, Friskus. Before we give up, let's take a last look
around."

All out of ideas, Sungi Bear's mom sits back down in her reading chair and says, "You win, Sungi Bear. Where are you?"

"Here I am Mommy!"
Sungi Bear reveals full of excitement.

Sungi Bear's mom smiles her biggest smile, walks over to Sungi Bear, and gives him a great big hug.

"Sungi Bear, you are the best hider ever! We looked everywhere... Where were you?" she asks.

Well, what do you know... Sungi Bear was sitting on his bed,
with his hands covering his eyes THE WHOLE TIME.
He was pretending to be invisible!

THE END

CPSIA information can be obtained
at www.ICGtesting.com
Printed in the USA
BVHW022038290621
610693BV00004B/14